STEVEN SPIELBERG PRESENTS

AN AMERICAN TAIL
FIEVEL GOES WEST™

FIEVEL'S JOURNEY

From a screenplay by Flint Dille
Story by Charles Swenson
Based upon characters created by David Kirschner

Grosset & Dunlap • New York

Little Fievel Mousekewitz sat by his apartment window and gazed out at New York City. But Fievel wasn't seeing the busy, crowded streets of the city. He was seeing the wind-swept plains of the West. Fievel loved cowboys and sheriffs and adventure. But most of all, the little mouse liked to imagine he was on the frontier too, fighting evil cats and being a real Western hero.

Fievel looked across the sooty rooftops and waved to his best friend, Tiger. Tiger was a cat—but he was sweet and good-hearted.

"Fievel, supper's ready!" It was Mama, calling him to dinner.

Fievel joined his family—Mama, Papa, Tanya, and baby Yasha. Mama looked around the table and sighed. "I wish there was more food."

Fievel patted his mama's hand. But before anyone could even take one bite of the little food there was, the sound of an alarm shook the tiny apartment.

It was a cat attack!

Quickly the Mousekewitzes hid inside a sardine can—
all except Fievel. He raced back to the window.
"Fievel!" shouted Mama. "Get in here with us."

But Fievel had already grabbed his hat and climbed out the window, onto the roof. Maybe he could be a Western hero right here in New York!

From high up on his rooftop perch Fievel saw a gang of cats chasing mice through the streets and down into the sewers. And there was Cat R. Waul, leader of the cat gang, with Chula the tarantula by his side.

"Come down, Fievel," cried Mama. She and the others had
followed Fievel to make sure he'd be safe.

Just then a cat leaped up onto the roof—right next to Fievel.

"Oh, no!" Fievel said as he jumped back and landed in an old tuna can someone had left behind. The can teetered for a moment, then began to roll.

"Come on," called Fievel to his family. One by one they jumped in the can too. Picking up speed, it rolled off the roof...down into the street...

and right between the bars of a sewer grating. But the mice weren't
safe yet!

   The can splashed down into raging waters. Fievel held tightly to
the tin-can boat as waves crashed over the side and the mice spun
around and around in the rough sewer sea.

Finally the waters grew calm. Up ahead the Mousekewitzes could
see a group of mice gathered around a strange-looking mouse
wearing a cowboy suit.

"Pardon me, ya'll," the cowboy was saying. "But it seems I have
some train tickets out West. Tickets to a place called Green River,

where there's plenty of cheese, bright sunshine, and"— he paused for
a moment—"friendly cats."

"Cheese!" Mama said. "Friendly cats!"

"Cowboys!" said Fievel. "Out West!"

Papa looked at their excited faces and bought five tickets. The
Mousekewitzes were on their way!

Tiger, meanwhile, had heard about the cat attack. Worried about his little friends, he hurried to the Mousekewitz home. But it was too late. All Tiger found was an empty apartment—and a note from Fievel telling him they were heading West to Green River.

Already on board the train, Fievel watched the countryside rush past as day turned into night. Soon the other mice fell fast asleep. But Fievel was still wide awake. He climbed onto a high beam and scurried from car to car, exploring every nook and cranny.

Suddenly Fievel saw a shape up ahead.

"Hey, I know you," he said. It was the strange cowboy mouse!

Fievel tapped the mouse on the shoulder. But the mouse tumbled forward with a lurch and tangled poor Fievel in its strings.

"It's a puppet!" said Fievel with a gasp.

Then the little mouse looked down and held his breath. Right below him a gang of cats was listening carefully as Cat R. Waul explained his evil plot.

"All the mice from New York City are on this train," he said, "just as I planned. And when we get to Green River we'll catch them all at once—in a giant mousetrap disguised as an outdoor theater. There will be mouseburgers for everyone!"

Fievel tried desperately to work himself free from the puppet strings. He had to warn the others. Cat R. Waul had been pulling the wooden mouse and doing its talking. The whole thing was a trap!

Just then Cat R. Waul plucked Fievel out from the strings and looked at him hungrily.

"Something must be done about this mouse," Cat R. Waul told Chula. "Throw him from the train!"

Chula gave Fievel a push and the little mouse landed, unhurt, on the desert sand.

"Don't worry," Fievel called to his family as the train chugged West. "I'll meet you in Green River." There was nothing to do but continue his journey—alone.

Fievel followed the railroad tracks across miles of empty desert. Suddenly a giant hawk swooped down and, lifting Fievel high into the air, carried him away.

The hawk flew for miles and miles until finally it dropped Fievel. Down, down, down the little mouse fell... right into a bowl filled with vegetables. Then Fievel saw a large set of teeth. They were about to close in on him!

Suddenly the teeth stopped moving. Then Fievel heard a familiar voice call his name. It was Tiger! He had followed Fievel all the way out West.

"Tiger! Am I glad to see you!" exclaimed Fievel. He told his best friend all about Cat R. Waul and his evil plans.

"You've got to help," Fievel pleaded.

Tiger agreed, and the two friends hurried to an old barn. There, Sheriff Wylie Burp—lawdog of Green River—was waiting to teach Tiger how to be a dog.

Wylie showed Tiger how to growl and bark and snap at a dummy made up to look like Cat R. Waul. Then Fievel dressed Tiger in a cowboy hat and dog tags. Tiger—the dog—was ready.

When Fievel, Tiger, and Wylie arrived in Green River a little while later, all the mice were filing into the outdoor theater. They still didn't know it was a mousetrap.

"Stop that cat. Quick!" Fievel said to Tiger. "He's about to cut the ribbon and release the trap."

    With Fievel and Wylie beside him, Tiger took care of the cats.
Snarling like a real dog, he twirled each one over his head like a
lasso and tossed the whole gang onstage.

    The mice realized they were sitting in a trap and fled the stands.
When the seats were empty, Fievel cut the ribbon. Snap! The stage
flipped up. Cat R. Waul and his gang were thrown high into the air,
then down onto a passing train. The mice were saved!

"Fievel!" shouted Mama, running over with Papa, Tanya, and baby Yasha to hug the little mouse. "You're a hero."

"Shucks, Ma," said Fievel, tipping his hat over one eye again. "'Twasn't nothing." Then he winked and grinned. Maybe he was a real Western hero after all.